THE CHRISTMAS GROOM'S INNOCENCE

MAIL ORDER BRIDES OF COLORADO

SUSANNAH CALLOWAY

Tica House
Publishing
Sweet Romance that Delights and Enchants!

PERSONAL WORD FROM THE AUTHOR

Dearest Readers,

Thank you so much for choosing one of my books. I am proud to be a part of the team of writers at Tica House Publishing who work joyfully to bring you stories of hope, faith, courage, and love. Your kind words and loving readership are deeply appreciated.

I would like to personally invite you to sign up for updates and to become part of our **Exclusive Reader Club**—it's completely Free to join! We'd love to welcome you!

Much love,

Susannah Calloway

VISIT HERE to Join our Reader's Club and to Receive Tica House Updates!

https://wesrom.subscribemenow.com/

CONTENTS

CHAPTER 1

The sound of a gunshot, echoing through the surrounding hills, woke George McDonald with a start. He lay for a few moments on his bedroll, listening for any other noise. But the only thing he heard from outside his little shanty was the quiet burble of the stream nearby.

He reckoned that it was some hunter or other. It wasn't all that unusual to hear a rifle. After all, out here in the middle of nowhere, each man had to fend for himself—and squirrels and the occasional deer were staples. Still, most of the prospectors that George knew of around the little mining settlement were trappers, rather than shooters. It was early in the day, too, scarcely even light yet. Much more common to go hunting in the evening, after twilight.

He shook the curiosity out of his head and got up from his bedroll, stretching tall and feeling his back pop and settle into place. After three months of prospecting here, he was about ready to call it quits, move on to somewhere else. It wouldn't be the first time.

At thirty-three, George had spent most of his life working hard to make a living. From the farm he'd grown up on, to driving a stagecoach, to prospecting, he wasn't afraid of turning in a long day's work. But he had to admit to himself – there was no one else around to admit it to – the thrill of the hunt was beginning to pall. More and more, he dreamed about what he would do with the gold that he found…if it ever happened.

"Buy a little farm someplace," he told himself, stirring up the coals in the fire pit outside the shanty. "Maybe even raise a family." The thought made him smile; it seemed as far off as striking it rich. "Ah, well…doesn't hurt a man to dream, does it?"

He did wonder, now and then, what it would be like to find a young woman who would consent to be his wife. She would be cheerful, calm, and industrious, as well a strong and caring. And if she was pretty, too, well, that was just icing on the cake. Maybe after he found a little gold…

But he knew full well he'd never find a woman who was willing to set up housekeeping in a little shanty in the mountains of Colorado, not on the strength of "maybe."

All that day, as he went about his business, his thoughts kept straying back to the gunshot he'd heard upon waking up. Upon reflection, it was doubly odd that there had been only one shot - unless the hunter had a very good aim, and got his prey with that first lucky one.

George found that he was more on edge through the day, half expecting to see a rifle-toting prospector show up on the area that he had staked out. There were occasional scuffles over claims; he'd had to walk away from more than one choice section of river in order to avoid violence. But this section was perfect; it was the place where the trickling stream joined the river, and the silt and rocks that were churned up by the turbulent waters were often speckled with nuggets and flakes of gold. He'd made enough to keep himself going, simply from panning. It was the way the water worked away at the nearby canyons, however, that was the most hopeful to him. He dug away at the small mine he'd started, with pick and axe and shovel, letting his dreams occupy his mind even as he kept an eye out for any interlopers.

Perhaps it was that heightened sense of alertness that caught his attention as he pulled his pick away from the rocks. If he hadn't looked closely, he might not have seen the seaming that led away from the direction he was digging. He might not have struck again, just to the left, and found that there was something a little softer and giving about the consistency of the rock face.

He might have entirely missed the gold seam that made his fortune and changed his life in a single day.

CHAPTER 2

Mr. Alfie Briggs stamped the title deed and shoved it across the counter to George McDonald. Along with it, he gave an effortless, friendly smile.

"Welcome to Shallow Gorge, Colorado," he said. "You chose a perfect time of year to buy."

The young man, scruffily bearded but with strong, noble features, folded up the paper and put it in his pocket. "That so?"

"Surely." Alfie nodded sagely. "We're just out of autumn, and winter comes early here in the valley. But it leaves early, too. I understand you've been living in the mountains a few hours north of here."

"Yes, since last spring."

"Well, I'm sure you'll find Shallow Gorge a pleasant change of pace. It's a small town, but I always say it's the jewel of Colorado. We've got two saloons, a hotel and two small inns, a town hall –"

George grinned at him. "Thanks, I took a tour before I decided to buy my property."

"Oh, of course you did. Do you mind me asking, Mr. McDonald – have you always been a farmer?"

George shook his head. "I was raised on a farm but haven't set foot in a farmhouse since I was a kid. Matter of fact, I'm looking forward to it. It's always seemed a peaceful sort of life for a man to have, farming."

"Mm. Hard work, though."

"I don't mind a little hard work. No man should. Or woman, either, come to that."

Alfie pushed his half-moon glasses a little further up on the bridge of his nose. "Indeed. Will your wife and family be joining you, Mr. McDonald? My wife would be delighted to have another young woman to chat with now and again."

In response to George's raised eyebrows, Alfie looked down at the counter and fidgeted with the cover on a ledger. "We're newly-weds, y'see…she's a little younger than I am. She'd like to have more friends, but there aren't many women here in Shallow Gorge. It's one of the town's only failings."

"I see. Well, the truth is, I ain't married." George put his hands palm-down on the counter and leaned on it, staring pensively downwards at the highly waxed wood. "And I guess maybe if I wanted to be married, this wasn't the place to come."

"Probably not," agreed Alfie. "Although, if you don't mind me giving you a little piece of personal advice…"

"Sure, go ahead."

"I happen to know that sending for an unmarried woman from places that are more highly populated with 'em has the potential to work wonders."

George blinked at him. "Come again?"

"Well, you see, my wife, for instance – she came out here to Shallow Gorge in response to a letter I wrote to a paper back east. She's from New York, originally."

"A letter?" said George thoughtfully.

"A Mail Order Bride advertisement," explained Alfie. "I wrote out a brief advertisement explaining that I was an unmarried businessman, looking for a wife, and unable to find one due to circumstances of life. Margaret wrote back to me, and we corresponded a few times, and then – well, now we've been married for two years, and I couldn't be happier."

George transferred his thoughtful glance to Alfie, who was, in fact, looking quite happy and pleased with himself.

"Hmm," he said.

"Just an idea," said Alfie. "If you're planning to stay in Shallow Gorge, you want to be married, and you don't have any eligible second cousins or whatnot, you could certainly do worse."

"I see. Well, I'll certainly think on it, Mr. Briggs. I could see getting lonely in that big house all by myself, and that's the truth."

"Especially on the long winter days and nights to come," Alfie urged him. "By the by, Mr. McDonald, do you mind me asking – how is that you made your money to buy a big property like Treehill Farm?"

"Mining," said George. "Gold mining. I believe the saying is, 'I struck it rich.'"

"Aha," Alfie said, beaming. "I had a suspicion that might be it. Well, I'll tell you what, Mr. McDonald, if you're going to write one of them letters like I did, I would include that little detail in there. I'm confident that it would catch attention."

George smiled at him. "I'm sure it would," he said. "I guess I'd better get on my way and inspect my new property, now. Thanks for your help, Mr. Briggs."

Alfie waved a hand at him as the younger man left, and leaned his elbow on the counter, contemplatively.

"Margaret will be so glad to have another friend move into town," he said, smiling to himself.

CHAPTER 3

On December the seventh, Mary Ferguson stepped down from the stagecoach and drew her coat around her shoulders a little more securely, shivering in the blast of cold air. Not that it hadn't been cold in the coach – it had – but there had also been other travelers, and walls to block out the wind. And she hadn't been standing ankle-deep in snow.

It was still snowing at the moment, the thick fluffy flakes coating everything in a clean white garment. Mary was used to snow; winters came early and stayed late in Vermont. But there, she had always been only a few steps away from a warm fire and a cup of tea. Here, she had no idea when she would find such comforts.

Or...*if* she would find such comforts. Suppose such things weren't in ready supply in Colorado.

She was being silly. Colorado was as much a part of America as Vermont. It wasn't a foreign country. They had discovered fire there. Tea, too, more than likely.

Still, she hoped that Mr. McDonald would be waiting for her at the inn, as he had said he would be in his last letter. There were all sorts of things that she could imagine going wrong —all sorts of things that would prevent him from coming to collect her. Her imagination did run wild at times; it quite got away from her, and especially in stressful situations. Such as this one – spending days traveling over the country, days in racketing, frigid coaches, days traversing over rough and bumpy roads, days spent thinking over the tragedies in the recent past and worrying over the possibilities of the imminent future…

A tall figure stepped up to her and touched his hat.

"Miss Ferguson?"

She looked up into his face and was conscious of a neatly-trimmed dark beard, a pair of deep blue eyes, kindly, with fine lines spreading out from them as though this man had done plenty of smiling in his lifetime.

"Mr. McDonald?"

"Yes," he said, beaming at her. He held out his arm for her to take and reached for her bag with his free hand. "Come along, miss, let's get you inside the inn and by a warm fire. There's a cup of tea waiting for you, too."

Mary sighed with relief and allowed herself to be led into the inn. In the late afternoon, the main room was half-full of travelers coming and going from the coach, and a few early dinner-goers waiting for the gong to be struck, calling them into the cold dining room for their meal. Mr. McDonald led her to an empty seat, just by the fire, and set her bag down at her feet.

"Now, you just warm up here for a minute, and I'll be right back."

She did as she was instructed, massaging some feeling back into her cold hands and stamping her boots a little to get the ice off her feet. She was feeling much better about everything by the time he came back and pulled up a little cushioned stool across from her. He sat down, a little awkwardly; his legs were far too long for him to be comfortable on such a seat, but he didn't look like the type to complain.

She was glad about that. Father had been a dear man, but he'd certainly been apt to nitpick more than his share. The last thing she needed after soothing him for the past twenty years was to find herself saddled with another fussy male. Now, she prided herself on her judgement of character. And going by the shy smiles George McDonald kept giving her, he was going to be no trouble at all.

Still, a girl could never be too cautious. She took a sip of the tea he had brought, regarding him curiously over the rim of the cup.

"I'm so pleased to meet you at last," she said finally. "I know we've only been corresponding for a few months, but it somehow seems as though I've known you for far longer."

"Oh, likewise," he said, blushing a little beneath his beard. "And I'm glad that you made it here safely, Miss Mary. How…how was your journey?"

"It was fine. A bit tiring, but I'm sure I'll recover before too long."

"Grand." He beamed at her for a moment. "Well, it's early enough in the day yet. I'd be happy to take you out to my land to show you around the place before we get you settled. That is, if you're feeling up to it."

"I feel up to anything," declared Mary. "I'm not about to let a little tiredness stand in the way. How far out of town is your land?"

"Oh, not far. Twenty minutes, maybe. I've got the buggy in the barn here, and Henry's all rigged up and ready to go. Henry is the horse," he added after a moment's thought, as though a bit worried that she wouldn't have understood that. His nervousness was actually quite endearing, and she smiled at him, hoping to put him a little more at ease.

"Then perhaps after I finish my tea." She glanced toward the door, which was bookended by a set of small windows with leaded panes. "You don't think the storm will be a problem with our travel?"

"The storm? Nah…just a little snow, that's all. I hear that blizzards don't come around here until January." His brows creased in anxiety. "You don't mind that there are blizzards, do you? The weather can get a little extreme…"

She waved a hand. "Not a problem at all, I assure you, Mr. McDonald. We had blizzards in Vermont, too."

"Oh, good." He nodded boyishly. "Please, call me George – if you don't mind."

"And you may dispense with the Miss – and call me Mary." She held out a hand, and he took it after a moment, holding it carefully. His hands were as warm as his smile.

"And maybe tomorrow," he ventured, "you can fill me in on what you'd like to do for Christmas. It'll be our first one together – it would be nice to make it memorable."

"Oh, yes." Mary could hardly credit it. Here it was, only a few weeks until Christmas; and by the time the holiday rolled around, she would be married. Married, to this unknown but sweet and friendly farmer sitting just in front of her. At times, the swiftness with which life moved boggled her mind. Just a few months ago, she had been sitting at her father's bedside in Vermont, comforting him in his last few hours. Now here she was, miles and miles away from everything she'd ever known, about to leap into matrimony with a complete stranger.

She supposed she should feel a bit more apprehensive. But now that she had met George, she felt that everything was, miraculously, working out according to plan.

All that remained was to see what alterations needed be made to the farmhouse, if any – and to order her wedding dress.

"A Christmas tree," she said. "We always had a tree back in Vermont."

"Oh, of course."

"And perhaps – I could cook a goose, or a turkey."

"Wild turkeys all over the place," he assured her. "Nothing simpler than to go out and shoot one."

"Oh, do you shoot?"

"Most of us do, here in Colorado. The stores are good for supplementals, you know, but if you want to eat meat during the winter, you'd best know how to provide for yourself and your family." He looked very earnest. Mary had always abhorred hunting, and guns in general, but she supposed that the environment called for it. She wasn't keen on giving up good food, either.

"All right, then," she said. "Perhaps that can be the beginning of our plan for Christmas together. And then, perhaps, in a few days…"

"Yes." The little touch of nervousness returned. "I suppose you're as anxious as I am to set a date. Well, I've got everything in order, so once you're happy with the house and any other things you want to get straightened out, I've already spoken to the preacher, and he's happy to let us use the church. I can have a few witnesses with a day's notice, too – Annie Borge, for example, she's my neighbor, and she's already told me she'd be happy to sit in on our nuptials."

"Your preparation is admirable. I'm happy to hear about it." She set her cup down on the little table beside her. "I'm quite warmed up now, George. If you're ready to go, I'm anxious to see my new home."

He beamed up at her.

"It's anxious for you to see it, too," he said, and leapt up from the little stool with a quickness that surprised her. He seemed very slow-moving, deliberate – the change took her aback a bit, but she decided that she liked the hint of impetuousness. Especially since it seemed to lead him to hold his hand out to her.

She took it and he led her back out toward the front door, carrying her bag along with him.

Just as they were about to exit, the door swung open inwards and a man entered, stomping small remnants of snow from his boots. He wore a black hat, which he took off and shook in the direction of the fire, sending water droplets flying. His eyes lit on George almost immediately, and the tight set of his mouth relaxed.

"There you are!" he exclaimed. "I thought I saw your buggy in the barn. Now, George, I don't want to make a big fuss over this, but I'm going to need to have a talk with you."

George halted and gave him a puzzled look.

"With me? What's this about, Sheriff?"

Sheriff Green folded his arms and cast a sideways glance at Mary.

"I don't like to air it in public, George. I think you'd really rather come into the sheriff's office with me and have it out there."

Mary shot a quick look at George, just in time to see him swallow hard. Underneath his beard, another slight blush was creeping up. She felt a sensation of uncertainty – George seemed to be an honorable man. She knew that he had lived in the area for only a short period of time. Could he already have gotten himself in trouble with the law?

And where did that leave her?

George turned to her now, almost as though she were his refuge.

"This is Miss Mary Ferguson," he said. "From back east, in Vermont. She's come in answer to my advertisement for a Mail Order Bride. She just arrived in town, and she doesn't know anyone."

"Why, good afternoon to you, Miss Ferguson," said Sheriff Green, though he hardly gave her more than a cursory glance before returning his gaze to George. "I understand your position, George, but be that as it may, we need to talk now. And given the circumstances, it's probably even more likely that you'll want to have this discussion in private."

George hesitated a moment longer. "Is it likely to be a while?"

"I can't really say. That depends on you."

A moment more, and he turned abruptly to Mary, placing a gentle hand on her arm.

"Please excuse me," he begged her. "And...don't worry. I'm sure that this will all work out. Do you mind waiting here for a little while?"

CHAPTER 4

Mary glanced around them at the entrance to the inn. There were a few other customers, and she felt more than a little embarrassed about the whole thing. She hated to think it, but it did not bode well for her relationship with George. At the same time, she was conflicted – she liked him right away, and she couldn't help but think that there must be a misunderstanding somewhere.

"I…suppose so," she said. "I can go and reclaim my seat by the fire and wait for you there."

"You do that." His hand still pressed on her arm, warm and reassuring despite the circumstances. "I'll be as quick as I can." He smiled at her but could not seem to meet her eyes. Turning away and leaving her in the hall, he followed Sheriff Green out into the cold.

Mary could see now that it was beginning to get dark. The sun set early this late in the year. Do you suppose he still expected her to go out and view the farm? She thought of traveling in the pitch black, in the cold, and shivered. She bent to pick up her bag, lugging the weight of it back toward the fire, and was taken aback when the burden was eased.

She looked up – and then she had to look down again.

A tiny, older woman had gripped the side of the bag and was helping her to carry it. She must have been near eighty years old, and a good few inches shorter than Mary herself, but she held onto the bag with a determination and strength that belonged to a much younger woman. She gave Mary a cheerful smile and hot-footed it over toward the fire.

"You must be the girl who came in answer to George's advertisement," she said, establishing Mary comfortably in her chair once more and crouching over the fire herself, rubbing her hands together to get them warm. She must have come from outside, but Mary hadn't even heard the door open. Perhaps she had been too preoccupied with the recent goings-on between George and Sheriff Green…

"Good! I was hoping to find you. Although I just saw George himself headed down towards the sheriff's office, along with Mike. What's happening there, my dear?"

She lapsed into inquisitive silence and peered at Mary with eyes like black seeds, nearly hidden behind wrinkles. For all her apparent age, her eyes were bright as a bird's, and her mouth seemed to relax into a permanent smile.

"I don't know," said Mary honestly. "I only just arrived, and we were about to go to George's farm when the sheriff came in – is it Mike? – and told him that they needed to discuss something. It must have been urgent, because he took George along with him right away."

"Ahh," said the elderly woman, thoughtfully. "Well, I'm certain it must have been something important…far be it from me to guess what. I suppose that I know George as well as any in these parts, but he is a newcomer, after all."

Mary stared at her, alarmed. "You think he might have done something to get him in trouble with the law?"

"George?" The old lady waved a hand. "Pish-posh. George wouldn't harm a fly. No, but he's the sort of person who might end up in a pickle, through no fault of his own. The sort that is easily taken advantage of, or wanders into things, simply because he's not paying enough attention. No, put your mind at ease, Miss Mary – it is Mary, isn't it? George said it was – he's perfectly innocent, I'm sure of it."

"Oh," said Mary, dubiously. "That's good."

"You're probably wondering who I am, aren't you?" The smile emerged and was displayed in full force. "My name is Annie Borge, and I'm George's nearest neighbor to the farm. I've got a farm of my own, just up the road and across the river from his. I say that I know him better than anyone here, and that's nothing but the truth. Not because George is the sort of man to open up to just anyone, mind you, but because I'm a born and raised busybody, and everyone knows it." She chuckled dustily. "I'm also the oldest woman in Shallow Gorge, so you can bet that I've seen it all."

Mary couldn't help but smile back at her. Annie Borge wasn't like anyone she had ever met, but she felt charmed by her.

"Well, I hope you're right," she said. "In the meantime, he asked me to wait for him here."

"Does he know how long it'll be?"

"The sheriff says it depends on him."

Annie frowned.

"Well, that could be forever and a day, for all we know," she said, discouragingly. "It's getting on for twilight. You don't want to be out in the winter dark, do you?"

"I certainly don't," Mary agreed readily. "You don't think that he intended me to stay with him on the farm, did you?"

"Of course not. He's a respectable man, and he wouldn't put you in that position. No doubt he was about to put you up here…" Annie glanced over at the man behind the counter, presumably the inn owner, for confirmation. His mouth set and stubborn, he shook his head. She changed her curious glance into a forbidding frown. "Now, what's this about, Nathan?"

"George might have mentioned it—might have said something about putting her up, but look. He's still a newcomer here, and I don't know him from Adam. I don't take credit from hardly anyone, and I'm not about to establish it with someone who was just carted off by the sheriff."

"Why, that's just…"

"That's all, Annie."

"Well, fine. Fine, then!" Annie stood up and put her hands on her hips. "You can just come home with me, Mary," she said, casting a spitfire glance toward the innkeeper. "I'll see that you're taken care of, and we'll just wait for George to return – no thanks to you, Nathan."

"Are you sure, Annie?" Mary said uncertainly.

"Why, I've never been more sure of anything in my life. Nathan can tell him where you've gone when he comes back – if we can trust you to do that much, Nathan – and he can collect you in the morning to show you the farm. We're really not far apart. It's the natural thing."

"Well…all right." Mary stood and picked up her bag once more. Annie took the other side of it to help and led her back out toward the front door, casting one last foreboding glance back at the irritating innkeeper.

"I'd like to say that the people of this town are more friendly than Nathan there," she said, as she led Mary to her waiting buggy. "The fact is, Shallow Gorge is as much at risk of uncaring types as any other place. Just because it's a small town doesn't mean that there aren't some big-town attitudes. Nathan is like that – born and raised here, but just as mean as they come and hard as nails. But take George, for example. He earned his money in a mine, from what I've heard, so he could be as snooty and prideful as you like, with what he's got. But he chooses to come to a small town and set up farming, in the hopes of leading a calm, peaceful life with a sweet wife by his side. It just goes to show that you never can tell about anybody."

She chattered on as she helped Mary into the buggy, and as they went on their way toward Annie's farm. Mary found herself relaxing under the incessant, calming influence of Annie's words. She was exhausted by the trip, and by the excitement of meeting George coupled with the uncertainty that had come afterward. When they arrived at Annie's farm, she was practically asleep on her feet.

CHAPTER 5

Sheriff Mike Green settled back in his chair and steepled his fingers in front of him, eyeing George. If he was trying to make the young farmer nervous, he was doing an excellent job of it. George swallowed hard past the lump in his throat.

He couldn't imagine why he had been called into the sheriff's office. And what a time to have this happen, when he had just met Mary in person. Poor girl, she must be wondering what on earth she had gotten herself into.

"Now, here's the thing, George," Sheriff Green said, still with that fixed-eye focus on him. "I heard not long ago that you came to us from a little settlement in the mountains to the north. Is that correct?"

George forced himself to speak.

"Yeah, that's about right. Last place I was at was called Dunnigan, after the first miner to strike gold. I was only there for about four months, though."

"That's where you struck it rich?"

"I wouldn't say rich," said George modestly. "But enough to buy my little farm, and a bit besides to keep me going until it's running like it should."

"Little, nothing," said Mike Green. "Your farm is well set to be one of the highest producing in the area, and I'm sure you know it."

"Well, everything I know about farming is from when I was growing up. I just hope I can keep it going and not run it into the ground. I aim to try, anyway."

"My point is, you made more than just a little and a bit up there in Dunnigan."

"Well, maybe a bit more than a bit."

"Ever hear of another miner up there named Shackleton? Albert Shackleton?"

"No, can't say I have. I didn't hang around much with the others. I was pretty solitary."

Sheriff Mike Green said, quietly, "You never heard about Shackleton's murder?"

George looked at him swiftly, eyes narrowed.

"Murder?"

"Shackleton was in Dunnigan the day before he was shot to death, talking about his new finds. He had the nuggets to prove it. Next afternoon, his brother comes to visit him at the mine and finds that he's been shot dead. It was clear that he had been digging, but the strain seemed to be exhausted and there was no gold anywhere in his camp. Not even the nuggets he had shown to highly interested observers just the day before."

Sheriff Green sat forward, hands on the desk between them. "Just a few days later," he said, "the assayer's office in the next town over records that a Mr. George McDonald has arrived, pounds and pounds of gold in tow. Apparently, this Mr. McDonald remained there in town instead of going back to his claim, even though he said that there was likely still more gold to be found. His claim happened to be nearby where Albert Shackleton had been mining – and where he was shot. Now, what I need to know, George, is this: you are that George McDonald in question?"

George's throat was dry. "Yes," he said hoarsely.

"Why did you leave your claim if there was more to be found?"

"I had enough. I had what I wanted – I was ready to spend it on my farm."

"Do you still deny that you knew Albert Shackleton?"

"I never met him. I never heard of him. I might have heard about a murder, but I wasn't still in Dunnigan at the time, so I didn't think much about it."

Sheriff Green sighed heavily.

"Well, those are the facts of the case," he said, "and as things lie right now, we have no major evidence against you, and I won't arrest you. But be assured, George, there's a manhunt on for the man who did this, and we will find him. If it turns out that you're lying – or even that you maybe know who did it and won't let on – I will find out. And then it won't matter whether your mother herself has just shown up on the stagecoach. Nothing will get in the way of me bringing you in. Understand?"

"I understand," said George.

Sheriff Green nodded at him in dismissal, and George found his way back out into the street. For some time, he walked, deep in thought, without really paying attention to where he was going.

Shackleton – had he heard the name before, and had it simply slipped his mind? No, he was fairly certain that he didn't know the man. And what had he heard about the murder in Dunnigan? The facts were very vague, as he recalled them. He'd heard more rumors than anything. But mining settlements were rife with robberies and violence – he hadn't thought much about it, apart from being glad that he was going to be living in a civilized area at last, having made enough of a fortune and being content with what he had.

It was clear that Sheriff Green found this difficult to swallow. What sort of man said, "I've found enough gold," and walked away from a healthy mining claim? But it was the truth, nonetheless. If only the people of Shallow Gorge knew him a little better and could vouch for him.

But no one knew him. He'd only been in town for a few months.

And, what was worse, no one could tell Mary Ferguson that he was trustworthy. He couldn't imagine what she must be thinking right now.

At the sudden remembrance of her, he stopped in his tracks and looked up at his surroundings, finding that he was on the other side of town from the inn where he had left her. He turned on his heel and began to make his way swiftly back. He'd lost all track of time – it was getting dark, and he still had to arrange with Nathan at the inn to make sure that Mary had a room.

To his surprise, Mary was nowhere to be found once he arrived back in the front room of the inn. On the other hand, he did find Nathan, wearing his typical sour expression.

"If you're looking for Miss Ferguson," he said, "I'm afraid you're out of luck."

George's heart sank. "She didn't get back on the coach, did she?"

"No, though I can't say as I'd blame her," said Nathan, polishing the little bell on the counter. "She was taken. Your neighbor took her home with her. I guess they want you to find her there."

"Oh!" George felt a surge of gratitude towards Annie Borge. She was a sharp old lady, and she must have come looking to meet Mary – and found a way that she could help. He was lucky to know someone like her. On top of that, she lived close to him, and he could drop by on his way home, make sure that Mary knew he hadn't been arrested.

"Thanks, Nathan. By the way, we spoke about arrangements for Miss Ferguson. Will you still honor her accommodations?"

Nathan frowned at him. "I hesitate to enter into business with someone who might be taken away by the sheriff at any moment," he said. "If you're willing to pay extra, up front, we might be able to reach an agreement. In the meantime…"

George shook his head. "Never you mind," he said. "I'll figure something out."

He left without saying goodbye, slamming the door behind him. Nathan. It was just like him, from what he'd seen of the innkeeper thus far. And Nathan wasn't the only one in town who seemed determined to make George continue to feel like an outsider. Would he ever feel as though he belonged in Shallow Gorge?

He was sure that the question about his history in Dunnigan was not going to help matters. But he couldn't do anything about that now – he could only continue to protest his innocence and hope that the law discovered the true culprit before his reputation suffered any more damage.

He drove the buggy toward his farm, turning down the lane to Annie Borge's house. Her farm edged up to one side of the river, and George's land started across from it, across a narrow bridge that was the only way across the water. At this time of the year, flush from the heavy rains of the fall, the river was still running strong. George knew that it would continue for another few weeks before it slowed down enough to freeze at the edges, and then start up again later, in the spring, when the snowmelt combined to swell the raging torrent once more.

Annie's house was a modest little place, and there was a light in the window. It was a welcoming sight, and George found himself smiling in anticipation as he clambered down from his buggy and knocked on the door.

Annie herself opened the door and peered up at him. "Aha! They set you loose."

George took his hat off respectfully. "I didn't ever really get arrested, Annie. Mike just had some questions for me."

"Is that a fact?"

"Yes, he –" George halted, unsure of how to explain himself. "He just...needed to ask me something." The last thing he wanted to do was alienate his closest ally here in Shallow Gorge – and he needed to decide how to explain it to Mary, too. That was what he was most anxious about. "Maybe this isn't the time to talk. May I come in and see Mary? I hear she came home with you."

"She did indeed, and no, you can't. Poor girl's worn out. I put her to bed, and I don't anticipate seeing her again this evening. You should head on home now, too, George, if you don't care to give me any explanations."

He hesitated again, wishing desperately there was an easy way to explain himself. But the words wouldn't come. It was too embarrassing – the idea that he was being investigated for murder. Even Annie would have a hard time standing up for him once she knew the truth.

"Well, all right," he said, stepping back from the door and already regretting that he was moving away from light and warmth, rather than toward it. "Can I come and collect her tomorrow morning? She wanted to see the farmhouse. But I understand it's late now, and she's tired."

"It's pitch dark out, and she's exhausted," Annie corrected him. "Yes, come back tomorrow, George. She'll be expecting you, I'm sure. I hope that you have a little bit better of an explanation for her, too – if I was her, I wouldn't buy what you told me for a minute."

Despite himself, George couldn't help but smile at his neighbor's forthrightness. He put his hat back on so he could tip it.

"I'll consider myself warned," he said. "Thank you for your help, Annie. I'll see you in the morning."

"Good night, George."

As he made his way back to his buggy and started towards his home, George realized that snow was beginning to fall once more. He wondered what tomorrow would bring.

CHAPTER 6

Mary awoke the next morning to sunny blue skies shining just outside the window, and the sound of water running in the distance. She kept still for a moment, bringing her mind around to where she was and what had happened yesterday. For a moment, it hovered just beyond her grasp, and she wondered if the noise she heard was her father, grumpily stoking the fire in the kitchen –

But no, she had made it Colorado, and the noise must be Annie because she was in Annie's house. Her father had been gone for months. The only man in her life now was… George.

She got up and found the washbasin in the corner and scrubbed vigorously at her face with a flannel to drive away the sleepiness. When she descended the stairs at last, she found Annie in the kitchen, turning bacon on the griddle, with a tea kettle just coming to a boil next to it.

"Ah, there you are, dear. Did you sleep well?"

"Like a baby," said Mary. "To tell you the truth, I was more exhausted than I even knew."

"I'm not surprised. I hear traveling will really take it out of you." Annie poured her a cup of tea and handed it to her, motioning for Mary to sit at the little kitchen table. "Go ahead and take a seat, and breakfast will be done in just a minute. Eggs, bacon, a little toasted bread, grits. It's what I was raised on, and I expect it'll suit you down to the ground. Tell me, Mary, after what happened yesterday, how do you feel about George McDonald?"

The frankness of the question took her aback somewhat. She sat down abruptly, half-dizzy with the memory of her worry and concern from the afternoon before.

"I don't think I feel any differently than I did before," she said after a moment. "I want to know what happened before I make any decisions."

Annie plopped two plates down on the table and sat down herself. "Good," she said firmly. "I think that's wise. There's no point in jumping to conclusions either way. And you'll be happy to know he came here to ask after you last night. You'd gone to bed already, or I would have come to let you know."

"Oh, did he?" Mary leaned an elbow on the table and picked up her fork. "I'm glad to hear that. I suppose if I'd awoken to find that he was in jail, or something like that, it would make the decision much easier."

"For you, maybe, but there are girls out there who would latch onto a man that much harder if he was in trouble with the law." Annie chuckled. "For one thing, some think it goes to show how tough they are. For another, a man that's in jail is far less trouble than a man who keeps stomping his muddy boots all over your floor. But to each their own. George will be along before too much longer, I expect. Hurry up and let's eat, otherwise he'll expect me to feed him, too."

Mary laughed, and the two women ate. In between bites, Annie asked questions about Mary's upbringing and her home in Vermont. Mary hadn't had a friend to speak to in many years, and she was unexpectedly touched by Annie's interest. It was especially moving to be able to speak with her about her father.

"You see, I don't have any other family members left," she said at last, "apart from maybe a distant cousin somewhere in Canada. I'm hesitant to throw my reliance on a tenuous relationship like that. When I saw George's advertisement, I thought it was as good a chance as any to start over somewhere new. And the letters that he sent were all very kind. He made sure to take an interest and ask about my history, and I found out a great deal about him, too..." She frowned thoughtfully. "Or, at least, I thought I did."

Annie patted her hand.

"Remember to wait before you make any decisions," she reminded her. "I think I hear Mr. McDonald's buggy in the yard this very moment, as a matter of fact."

To her own confusion, Mary found that George's arrival brought an answering blush to her cheeks. She stood hurriedly and began to help Annie with the dishes, hastening to busy herself until the knock sounded on the door. Annie gave her a knowing glance and went to let George in.

The young farmer followed Annie back into the warm kitchen, clapping his hands together to get the blood flowing back into them. He hailed Mary with a shy smile.

"I'm sorry I couldn't speak to you last night," he said. "I understand you were tired and had gone to bed."

"Yes, that's so. Annie has been very kind to let me stay with her."

"Oh – about that – I had set it up with Nathan for you to stay at the inn. Only…"

"Never mind about that," Annie broke in bossily. "I wouldn't send a dog I liked to stay with that man. Mary can just stay with me until the time comes. I've plenty of room and we're not far from your own homestead, George, so I don't imagine that you'll have a complaint."

"Surely not," said George, grinning at his take-charge neighbor. "That would be very kind of you, Annie. And…I hope we won't need your kindness long."

He cast a glance at Mary, and she was not surprised to see the questioning look in his eyes. She met his gaze steadily but could give him no answer.

"Nonsense," said Annie, shooing them both toward the door. "Everyone always needs kindness. Now, you two had best get along and look the farm over. I'm sure there'll be a few things need mending and adjusting, after a wifely inspection. And the weather looks threatening."

"It's a beautiful day, Annie," George protested. "The nearest clouds are miles off."

"They move faster than you might think, George McDonald. I've seen a few more storms come through these parts than you have, I'll warrant. Get on your way, you two young ones. I'll have some supper for you when you get back."

George caught Mary's eye as they were ushered out the door, and she couldn't help but return his smile. Once they were alone together, however, with the door closed behind them and the sunny day ahead, she felt a resurgence of her initial shyness.

This would never do, she told herself briskly. It was obvious that George was the shy type, as well. If they were both plagued with the same inability to say what they wanted to say, why, they'd never get anywhere at all.

She marched forward and held a hand out, waiting for George to help her up into the buggy. He did, readily enough, and hustled around to the other side to get up himself. Side by side, they drove the buggy back down the lane, the wheels crunching now and then over the freshly fallen snow.

"What do you think of Shallow Gorge so far?"

Mary looked about herself and took in a deep breath of the clean, frigid air.

"It's beautiful," she said simply. "I had hoped it would be. Vermont has its charms, of course – but nothing quite like this." The mountains in the distance were magnificent—stunning, even. She could see the clouds George had spoken of, rolling lazily over the foothills in their direction. But at the moment, the sun was so bright that she could almost convince herself she felt a little warmth from it, as weak as it was.

She was tempted to bring up the sheriff's questions from the day before. But the day was young, and there was a lot to do. Besides, it was pleasant just riding along at George's side, looking out at the gorgeous landscape, trying to make herself believe that she was really here in Colorado.

"Tell me about your past," she said.

George swallowed in what appeared to Mary's discerning eyes to be a nervous manner.

"Oh, you know everything there is to know about me," he said. "I wrote about it in the letters. Grew up on a farm – that's why I ended up here, with my farm now."

"Yes, but you made a few stops in between, didn't you? I mean to say, you didn't go directly from your farm to this farm. You were a prospector, weren't you?"

George wiped at his forehead. "Yes," he said, "I was."

"That's so exciting. I've never met a prospector before you. I suppose there's not a lot of gold in Vermont."

"I guess not."

"Will you tell me a little about it?"

George was quiet for a moment, as though trying to decide exactly what to say.

"It wasn't an easy life," he said, "but it was nice and silent out there in the wilderness, far away from anyone else. I don't think you'd care much for it. It ain't a place for a respectable woman to be."

"Were there no other people there, then? No town?"

"A settlement," he acknowledged. "Nothing more than that. Hey, look up ahead, Mary – there's my bridge."

She turned from her contemplation of his expression and looked ahead as she was bid. Indeed, the road now led to the left, splitting off from the main path, and there was a rickety-looking log bridge set low above the water. It was so low, in fact, that the rushing swells were nearly swamping it.

"Goodness! Doesn't it flood when it rains?"

"Hasn't yet," said George, and laughed when he saw her expression. "Well, keep in mind I've only been here a few months. I'll probably have to work on it, but the truth is, I've had to work on pretty much everything in this homestead, so I don't expect any different. But here we go, now."

She held her breath until the buggy was safely over the bridge and on the other side.

"Welcome home," said George shyly.

The farmhouse was far larger than she had pictured. It was rustic, to be sure, but there was a beauty in its simplicity; the raw wooden logs were tightly joined together, and even though she was no expert, she could tell that it was built to withstand anything the weather threw at it. There was a deep veranda running the entire length of the house, with two rocking chairs just waiting for occupants. A matching barn stood in the distance, with another two smaller outbuildings even further away.

"George. It's beautiful."

"Well, I'd like to take credit," he said, grinning, "but the fact is, that place was here long before I came around. I bought the farm from an older fellow who moved out to live with his daughter someplace in the east. He grew corn and sold it all over the county. I could do that. I've got a handful of cows, and space for hundreds. Or I could turn it into a pure cattle ranch. I haven't decided for sure what I want to do. Mostly I just like living on a farm."

His frank confession was just as endearing as his obvious nervousness had been the day before after they had first met, and she smiled widely at him as he helped her down from the buggy.

"I can see why," she said.

He led her into the house and followed her about as she walked through the front sitting room, back sitting room, kitchen, and then upstairs into each of the four bedrooms. The house was far larger than she had ever expected it to be. She thought momentarily that she wasn't sure she was up to the challenge but shook the thought off just as quickly. Of course, she would be. She'd always done anything she set her mind to.

That was what had gotten her this far to begin with.

At the end of the tour, he led her into the kitchen and established her in one of the straight-backed wooden chairs at the little table, then put the kettle on to make them both some tea. She was grateful for it; although they had been inside, few of the fires were going at this time of day, and the temperature outside seemed to have dropped dramatically.

"Well?" he said, setting her teacup down in front of her and taking a seat across the table. "What are your thoughts?"

"Oh, George, it's a wonderful place. I can see what drew you to it. I've never lived on a farm, myself, but I understand the appeal. And the surroundings are simply beautiful."

He was blushing again.

"Well, I'm glad that you like it," he said. "If you're happy, I'm happy. Is there anything you want to change? Anything I can do to make it more your home?"

The sweetness of this suggestion made her stop and smile at him.

"Well, I truly appreciate your care and attention. I'll have to think on it, I believe. It's all so much to take in – I can't make any decisions now."

"Oh." His face fell a little, and he looked down at the tabletop and drew his finger along the grain of the wood, pensively. "Does that mean…does that include setting a date for our wedding, too?"

She took a deep breath.

"George, what did the sheriff want with you yesterday?"

He looked up swiftly, and she could see the indecision in his eyes. Whatever it was that had happened the day before, he couldn't make up his mind whether he was going to tell her or not.

The thought left her colder than the weather outside, despite the warmth of the teacup in her hands.

There came a shout from outside. The look of relief on George's face made Mary's heart ache. He stood up from the table so quickly that he nearly knocked over his own cup of tea.

"Sorry, Mary," he said. "I'll be right back. Can't imagine who that might be."

Before she could say anything else, he was gone. Mary supposed sadly that it was all right – she couldn't think of what to say, anyhow.

CHAPTER 7

What a time for a distraction. George charged through the house, determined to thank whoever it was that had shown up at such an opportune moment. Yes, he would have to confess everything to Mary – as little as there was to confess – but the more he thought about it, the more it worried him that she wouldn't believe him if he protested his innocence. Sheriff Green had admitted that there wasn't enough evidence to hold him. But there was obviously enough evidence to cast him in the light of suspicion – and Mary didn't know him well enough to put any trust in him yet, no matter whether Annie was on his side or not.

He wrenched open the front door, caught sight of who was there, and slowed down immediately. He wasn't about to thank someone like Johnny Olsen, no matter what service the man had done for him.

Johnny Olsen was the epitome of everything George disliked about a person. For every honorable man like Sheriff Green, there was a back-stabbing Nathan; for every kind, honest neighbor like Annie Borge, there was a mean, twisty Johnny

41

Olsen. What made matters worse was that Olsen was also a near neighbor; not quite as close as Annie, but he was further down the main road, on the same side of the river as Annie was. The man had no reason to have crossed George's bridge, and no reason to be standing there in his yard now.

Still, George was nothing if not polite. He stepped out of the house and advanced to the edge of the veranda, noting that the clouds had come a great deal closer. Annie was right, after all.

"Johnny," he said levelly.

Olsen waved at him. He was still astride his gray pony, which was prancing nervously under his hand.

"You'll want to have that bridge looked at by someone who knows what they're doing," Olsen told him. "You can't have structures like that around here – they're a danger to society."

"Society shouldn't be trespassing on my land," said George. "No one has any call to cross that bridge but me, and I don't think it's on the verge of collapsing. What can I do for you, Olsen?"

Olsen got down from his horse and walked forward, tugging it by the reins. Once he was at the foot of the veranda steps, he stopped and looked up at George, eyes narrowed.

"Not a very kindly way to greet a neighbor," he said. "Especially one who came here specially to help you out."

George sighed. "Thanks for the warning about the bridge, Johnny."

"Now, that's not what I'm talking about, and you know it."

"I don't know any such thing. What did you come here to tell me?"

Olsen stepped onto the first of the steps, that much closer to George. This close, he reeked of the tobacco he habitually chewed, and George could see just how stained his teeth were.

"Sheriff Green's out to get you," he said, loudly and clearly. "You'd best watch out."

George took a step back, but it didn't help to distance him any, as Johnny Olsen immediately came up the remaining two steps onto the veranda.

"I spoke with the sheriff yesterday. It's just a misunderstanding."

"Misunderstanding? Poor guy gets shot and is found out in the woods with everything he owns stolen from him – that's not a misunderstanding, that's a complete tragedy. It's a job, George – and Mike's sure that it was your hand that did the work. Now, I'm not saying whether he's right or not – far be it from me to judge. I don't know you, and you don't know me. But I can tell you this: if the law enforcement from Dunnigan asks Mike for a favor, he's going to see that he gets it done."

"I don't know what you mean."

"I mean that Mike can't afford to alienate anyone, not when he's running for reelection next year. If a neighboring sheriff asks him to turn over a suspect, especially someone who's already been named as the killer, Mike's not going to play favorites. You're done."

"Who would name me?" George shook his head. "I didn't do anything wrong."

"That's what they all say."

"I don't even know anyone in Dunnigan."

"Well, sure, now that Shackleton is dead," said Olsen pragmatically. He scratched the back of his hatless head. His hair was black as pitch, thick as a forest, and it was so long that the fringe of it hung into his eyes. George had never seen anyone quite like Johnny Olsen. And he never wanted to see Olsen himself ever again; the entire conversation was a nightmare. But he didn't know how to escape it.

"But like I said, I'm here as a concerned neighbor, trying to help you out."

"How, exactly?"

"Look, Mike's not going to stop until he finds enough to lock you up. And once he does that, everything you own is fair game. Even if they decide that you're innocent and let you free, it'll be months – years, maybe. Your farm will sit here and rot, fall away in pieces. Squatters will come in. You'll lose everything you've got. It's inevitable, George."

George had a bitter taste on his tongue. "What are you suggesting?"

Olsen smiled slight, crooked smile.

"I'm suggesting that you let me, your neighbor who has your best interests at heart, help you out. Sign your property over to me, and I can take care of it for you."

"In exchange for a hefty percentage of it, I guess."

He waved a hand. "Nonsense. What would I do with a big ranch like this, on the other side of the river from my land? Listen, if you felt moved to reward me for my friendship, I'll leave that up to you. Other than that, I'm just here out of the goodness of my own heart."

George set his jaw firmly.

"You want me to sign my land, that I just purchased with my hard-earned money, over to you in the hopes that you'll do the honorable thing and just deed it back to me, when it's time?"

"When it's time," said Olsen. "That's exactly right."

George shook his head. "I don't know you very well, Johnny, but I'm pretty darn sure that you didn't come here out of any goodness of your own heart. Mostly because I doubt that there's any goodness in there to spare. Get off my property."

He saw the color drain from Johnny Olsen's face, and the thought crossed his mind fleetingly: have I made a mistake? Have I made an enemy?

"Keep in mind," said Olsen levelly, "that I don't know you too well neither, McDonald – none of us here in Shallow Gorge do. You're a stranger to us, and when the sheriff comes asking questions about where you were when a man was murdered, well – it's enough to make a body wonder. You've got little enough reputation here, George. I'd hate to see what there is of it be tarnished forever."

George took a quick step forward, and Olsen backed off, backing down the steps and moving toward his horse.

"I'll see myself out," he said, swinging up into the saddle. As he started to ride off, he shouted back over his shoulder, "And take a look at that bridge before someone gets killed."

As his angry neighbor rode off into the gathering gloom, George stood and watched him disappear. His thoughts churned, none of them making any sense. Olsen hadn't a kindly bone in his body; there was absolutely no chance that he was truly acting in anything other than his own self-interest. But what did he want with George's land? And how did he know what happened the day before with the sheriff? The idea that the rumor mill in Shallow Gorge was already busily churning made George's stomach twist.

He'd scarcely been here three months. Was he doomed to endure the sideways looks, the quiet whispers, the ceaseless gossip of Shallow Gorge for the rest of his life – or until he gave up his beloved property and left the area?

The mountains in the distance were almost completely hidden from view. From far away, sweeping down on the valley like a heavy curtain, the rain was coming.

CHAPTER 8

George was still standing outside, looking after the man he had called Olsen. But he could return at any moment, and if he opened the door and caught Mary standing in the front sitting room, he would realize that she had heard everything.

Everything.

She held her breath and tiptoed back into the kitchen, regaining her seat. Though she tried to rearrange herself in the same position as she had been when he left, she realized when she gripped her teacup that her hands were shaking badly. He would know something was up. She dropped them into her lap just as George came back into the kitchen.

He heaved a deep sigh at the sight of her waiting for him.

"It was a neighbor," he said. "Lives back across the bridge and down the road."

"Oh?" She did her best to sound nonchalant. "What did he want?"

"He wanted…to warn me about the bridge."

"The bridge?"

"Yeah, my bridge." He gave a weak smile. "I told him that my best girl had already given me a stern warning about it, and I'd take a look at it to make sure it was safe."

"Oh." Her frown of consternation was real. If the bridge broke, she would be stranded on one side or the other – on Annie's side, unable to get to George, or on George's side… unable to get away from him. Either way, she didn't like the sound of it.

He picked up on that readily enough. "Don't you worry," he said. "It's going to be fine. I've driven across that bridge time and time again. And I'll keep an eye on it if the water gets any higher." He reached out a hand to her, and she took it, letting him help her stand up from her seat. "Speaking of which, the rain's about to hit. I'd best get you back to Annie's, or you'll be spending the night here."

He paused, as what he had suggested hit him with full force, and their eyes met for a brief, shy moment, before they both looked away, sharing an identical blush. But George kept possession of her hand as he led her back through the house – and she let him.

What she had heard through the front door of his log farmhouse had been muffled and unclear, but she had certainly heard enough to make her wonder. It was something about the sheriff coming to arrest him – and something about a murder. Could it really be so? George seemed so sweet, so honest, so honorable. Could he really have done something so dastardly?

And the neighbor, the man called Johnny Olsen – she hadn't even caught sight of him, but she disliked him intensely. It was something about the oily way in which he spoke. There was something more going on than he admitted to. If it came down to a question of whether to believe Olsen or whether to believe George, well – she knew which she would choose.

But that didn't mean she shouldn't be careful. After all, she'd only just met him.

It was a relief that he was taking her back to Annie's house. They didn't speak much on the way, other than a quick discussion on what supplies he needed to get for the house, especially for the upcoming Christmas Day celebration. She was having a hard time imagining Christmas without her father, but she needed to get used to the idea. Not only was she going to spend a Christmas in Colorado, but she might be spending it as a married woman.

As he left her at Annie's door, handing her down into the yard, George held onto her hand for a moment longer than was absolutely necessary, looking deeply into her eyes.

"We'll set a date sometime soon, won't we?" he said.

She couldn't help but meet his gaze, and once she did, she found that she couldn't look away. There was no doubt about it: George McDonald was an attractive man, for all his shyness and mystery. Indeed, perhaps it was his shyness and mystery that made him so attractive to begin with.

She nodded. "Sometime soon," she agreed. *As soon as I make up my mind whether to marry you or not, in fact.*

"Good. And tomorrow, maybe you'd like to come with me in the afternoon, head out into the hills. I'd like to get a small Christmas tree for the house."

Fixated by his eyes, she couldn't do much more than nod. She was a little afraid of what might come out of her mouth if she tried to speak. She had never stood this close to a man before, not for this long of a moment, and he was overwhelming her defenses.

At last, though he hesitated, the oncoming rain forced him to release her hand and her gaze.

"Sleep well, Mary," he said. "Tell Annie I'm sorry I couldn't come in for supper, but if I'm going to get back and check that bridge before it gets dark, I'd best get a move on."

She ran to make it to the porch before the first few drops of rain fell, and she watched him as he trundled the buggy back down the lane, heading home. Then, at last, she went inside and found Annie in her kitchen, already pouring a cup of tea.

"Here you are, dear. Did you have a nice time? That farmhouse is more than you expected, isn't it?"

"It's certainly something." Mary accepted the tea with a murmur of thanks, and sat down at the table, bending over the cup to inhale the hot steam greedily. It was only a ride of about ten minutes or so between George's house and Annie's, but the temperature had dropped steadily over the course of the day, and she was freezing. "I can just picture it with a woman's touch."

"Aha. And you and George got along?" Annie sat down next to her.

"We did. He's a kind man. And a perfect gentleman, from what I can tell."

"And did he tell you what the sheriff wanted to talk to him about?"

Mary looked down at the teacup, feeling yet another blush warm her skin. She searched for the words she wanted, and finally settled on, "Not entirely. He was about to, but – I believe it's something about a crime that was committed."

Annie gave a short bark of a laugh. "Well, I'd hardly expect anything other than that, since the sheriff took him in for questioning. Mike hardly ever brings anyone in for anything other than a crime. You don't get a lot of sheriffs asking you to come down to the law office for helping an old lady across the street, for instance."

Embarrassed, Mary couldn't help but smile at Annie's sharp humor. "I'm sure he'll tell me when he's ready," she said, wondering why she already felt compelled to defend the man.

Annie examined her closely for a moment, and then nodded.

"And yet, you've already decided that you're going to marry him."

"What? I haven't decided any such thing. I decided to wait until I found out."

"Say what you like, but I know infatuation when I see it," said Annie, settling back in her chair comfortably and taking a genteel sip of her tea.

"I'm not infatuated. I am simply…intrigued."

"Sounds like a fancy eastern word for puppy love, if you ask me."

There was clearly no getting around Annie's opinions; they expanded to take up the whole room. Mary settled for shaking her head and giving a half-hearted chuckle.

"Anyway," she said, "he's going to take me with him to find a Christmas tree tomorrow."

"Grand," said Annie dryly, "he'd never be able to manage it on his own, I'm sure."

CHAPTER 9

It was well after lunch time when George arrived the next day, smiling his gentle smile and obviously raring to go. He suffered himself to be brought in and given a cup of tea against the looming weather.

"But it's another beautiful day outside," he pointed out when Annie told him that the tea would ward off the cold. "The sunlight sparkling off the snow is blinding."

"I was right yesterday," Annie said dogmatically, "and I'll be right today. You mark my words."

She sent them on their way with a flask of hot coffee for later on. "You'll need it."

George had brought a rough-hewn farm cart instead of his smart little buggy. He spread a fur rug over Mary's knees, and another around her shoulders. Comfortably wrapped in fur, sitting at his side, she was quite warm and cozy, though the air was certainly brisk, to say the least.

"Have we far to go?"

"Yeah, it's a fur piece," George joked, tapping her shoulder. She shook her head, not sure whether to roll her eyes or laugh – but that would surely only encourage him! – and he clucked to his horse, the cart rolling away down the lane.

"It's about an hour to the foothills," he said. "There's a nice little stand of firs there. I happened to see it shortly after I moved here, when I was exploring the countryside. We should be able to find a suitable tree in that little grove. I don't want anything too large, of course."

"Of course," said Mary. "Heaven forbid that you fit anything too big in your tiny house. You simply wouldn't have the room."

He shot her a quick glance, dubious at first, and then relaxed when he realized she was joking, and even went so far as to laugh. He didn't seem to feel any compunction about encouraging her silly humor, she was rather grateful to find.

The drive out to the fir stand was lovely, since she was warm enough. The skies were a startling blue, the sun dazzled off the snow into a million diamonds everywhere she looked – and the man sitting near her was handsome and warm and kind. For the first time in a long time, Mary felt quite content.

Once they arrived at the area he had sought, she was happy to find that the foothills were equally lovely as the valley, although in a different way. He handed her down and showed her what sort of tree to look for.

"Not too big now, remember."

"Oh, I certainly will."

Arm in arm, they headed off through the snow, which was more than ankle-deep. He kept careful hold on her to ensure that she didn't sink too far, she was pleased to note.

It took some time – longer than she had expected, certainly, and longer than he had thought, she suspected. He left her standing beside the little tree, shaking snow from its boughs, while he returned to the cart, bringing back a sharp axe which he'd forgotten. Watching him cut the tree down was fascinating. He had taken off his coat to get a better, more uninhibited swing, and she could see the muscles of his back working beneath his dark blue shirt with each movement.

When the little tree was felled at last, he stood and wiped the sweat off his forehead, catching her looking at him.

He grinned at her, and she blushed, looking away.

"Now comes the hard part," he said.

Never one to back away from a challenge, Mary helped him carry and then lift and push the trunk of the tree deep into the back of the wagon, securing it with ropes. Their physical labor over, they sat in the driver's box and she retrieved the flask of coffee from beneath the seat, pouring him a draught into a tin cup. They sat together in companionable silence, looking out over the valley.

George finally broke the silence, looking into the depths of his coffee cup.

"You like it here in Shallow Gorge?"

She looked for the right words to say.

"Well, it's only been a few days, thus far," she said. "But – yes. I like it, what I've seen. Annie is sweet. The town is beautiful. And you… are you."

He looked up at her, and she made sure to smile at him, letting him know without saying in words that she had meant to be encouraging. Flattering, even.

He smiled back.

"I'm glad to hear it," he said. "I'm still trying to figure out how I feel about it, myself. I love my farm, I love the promise of it, what it can be someday. Annie's a kick, right enough. And there are good people here in Shallow Gorge." His face darkened a little. "But there are bad people, too."

"That's true of anywhere," Mary said. "It was true in Vermont, it's true in Colorado, and it's true in California. You can't escape that, no matter how hard you try. You can only focus on the good people, when you find them."

George nodded, eyes distant, and then she realized that the warmth on her gloved hand was his, bare and ungloved, curling lightly over her fingers.

She let him hold her hand, and they sat for a moment longer without saying anything. Then he took a deep breath.

"Mary…"

"Yes," she said quietly. "Yes, George McDonald, I will marry you. Tell me when to be in church, and I'll see you there."

He squeezed her hand, and she thought for a moment that perhaps he would kiss her. But his shyness won out over any motion he might have made, and he let her go at last and picked up the reins instead.

"We'd best be getting back," he said, squinting at the sky. "Looks like snow's on the way."

She moved a little closer to him, just close enough to feel the side of his shoulder pressing warm against hers and nodded. "All right. I'm ready."

The snow was, indeed, on the way, and it caught up with them faster than either of them expected. They had just trundled over the bridge – which made a worrying noise, Mary noted, a noise she didn't remember from before – and they were about to pull up in his yard when the skies unleashed.

He leapt out.

"Stay here just a moment," he said. "Guess it wasn't such a good idea to bring the tree home and set it up tonight. I'll haul it out in a jiffy, and we'll get you back to Annie's for the night."

"Why not leave it and get it out later?" she asked, turning around in the seat to watch him.

He shook his head. "I don't like the extra weight going over the bridge," he said. "I just checked it yesterday – it's sound – but you heard that creaking as well as I did, I'm sure."

"Yes."

"Hold on just a second, Mary."

It was, in fact, a little more than a second before he had wrestled the tree out of the back of the cart. Meanwhile, Mary sat bundled up in her furs, wanting to help, but suspecting that he would worry so much about her that she would be in the way. The skies continued to unleash their furies, a silent, beautiful, deadly fury – she knew about snowstorms and blizzards.

"If we get back to Annie's," she called to him, "you may have to stay."

"I'll figure it out once we get there," he called back, breathing heavily. At last, he had rolled the tree up onto the veranda, and returned at a trot to the cart, slapping the reins on his horse's back and getting the cart to jolt into action. "Hang on tight, Mary, we're going to go a little quicker this time."

She didn't need any second urging.

The bridge was before them, and she felt a moment of unease as they clattered onto it. But it held, and they were already halfway across. Perhaps this fast movement was better than going over it slowly. She didn't even hear any creaking.

The bridge gave way in a terrible, awful silence, blanketed by the falling snow, crashing down into pieces. The only noise came from the cart splashing into the water, the shrieking of the startled horse, and a yelp and a scream from both Mary and George, quickly drowned out by the frigid river.

Mary was lost. She could not tell down from up; her eyes felt as though they were frozen shut, frosted over. Everything was dark, and everything was cold. Everywhere, there were splashes and the sound of water running, and she felt the bulk of something huge and solid pass just near her – the horse! – and then it was gone again. She could not breathe, and then she could, and then she could not again, and she opened her mouth to take in another breath and there was nothing but water.

Suddenly a strong hand seized her by the collar and dragged her bodily up out of the water, one mighty heave, and then another, and another, until she was completely free of the river and lying high up on the bank, with George's white, panicked face hovering over hers.

She blinked at him, and he breathed a soft prayer of thanks and leaned over her, pressing his lips to her forehead. Mary felt that she could have rested there forever, out of the water, with George near, although even his lips were cold. Everything was cold.

But he was making her get up, right quick-like, regardless of what she wanted.

"We've got to get you warmed up," he said. "You've got to stand, Mary. We'll get back to the house, out of the snow."

"The horse…"

"She's fine, Mary. The cart smashed in the fall, and the harness came loose. She's just there, downstream, see?" He pointed, and sure enough, Mary could see the mare busily shaking herself loose of the last of her tack. "Come along, sweetheart, everything's going to be fine."

It was such a wonderful thing to hear – everything's going to be fine – that Mary allowed herself to be led back to the log farmhouse, brought inside, and placed by a fireplace in the kitchen. She was vaguely aware that George was feverishly stirring up the coals, stoking the fire, making it roar. The warmth was beginning to seep back into her when he stopped in front of her suddenly and took her by the shoulders.

He looked embarrassed.

"Mary…"

"George?"

"You're going to need to take off your clothes. They're soaking wet, and you'll catch your death. Can you do it on your own?"

She nodded slowly. He eyed her for a moment, then he nodded, evidently convinced.

"Good," he said, clearly relieved. "I'll go and do the same myself. I've put some blankets here for you to wrap yourself in. I'll come back once you're done and covered and fix us something hot to drink. All right? All of your clothes, mind. Don't leave anything." Mary was oddly amused to see that he was blushing, yet again. He gave her one last stern look and rushed out of the room, closing the door behind him.

Alone in the now warm kitchen, Mary undressed and swathed herself in blanket after blanket. She seated herself in front of the fire once more and basked in the warmth as the chill slowly seeped out of her. The day had been…well, the day had been topsy-turvy, quite frankly. From uncertainty about George, to accepting his proposal of marriage, to a collapsing bridge… she was fairly certain that nothing like this would ever have happened back in Vermont.

There must be something special, something different, about Colorado. From the spunky, sharp neighbor to the shy, perplexing man she had this afternoon agreed to marry, there just seemed to be more *life* here.

The thought needed some serious contemplation. She contemplated it so deeply, in fact, that she fell fast asleep.

CHAPTER 10

Mary was awakened by the sunlight streaming into the kitchen. For a moment, she sat still and blinked, trying to reconcile her surroundings with what she remembered. Suddenly, the previous day came back to her in a rush, and she sat up with a gasp, clutching the blankets tightly around her.

She was in a different chair, a little armchair that George must have moved in by the fire. The blankets were just as tightly wrapped as they had been the night before, she was glad to see. Hung out before the still-roaring fire were her clothes, now warm and dry. She reached for them, blushing at the thought of him lifting her in the night and moving her.

She must have been sleeping more heavily than she realized. And now, here she was, in his kitchen, and he was probably waiting for her to awake so that he could have his breakfast and coffee. Was there any way that things could get more awkward?

Mary should have known better than to even pose the question to herself, for just at that moment, she heard a far-away knock. Someone was at the front door.

She froze, and heard footsteps above, heading down the staircase. There were voices at the front door, too muffled to understand. In a great hurry, she dressed herself, and carrying her shoes in her hand, peeked out the door of the kitchen.

The visitor was Sheriff Green. Anxiety gripped at her insides – what would the sheriff think, finding her here alone this early in the morning? – but it was too late. He had already seen her, and his puzzled, inquisitive expression alerted George, who turned around to see her.

"Oh, Mary. You're awake."

She could tell by the blush on his cheeks underneath the beard that he, too, was aware of how this must look. He turned back to Sheriff Green.

"Like I was saying, Mike, it happened just as it was getting dark, so there was no chance of getting through to the other side. I'm just glad that Mary is all right."

He gestured for her to enter the sitting room, and she did, twining her hands together nervously.

Sheriff Green regarded her seriously.

"I'm glad of that, too," he said. "It could have been very dangerous indeed. You need to keep an eye on that bridge, George."

"Too late now," said George. "I'll have to rebuild it. But the fact of the matter is that I had just reinforced it last week, and double-checked it yesterday, and the day before. It showed a few signs of weakness, so I shored it up even more. It should have been stable as a rock; I don't know how on earth it ended up collapsing. There wasn't that much water coming through."

"How did you get across?" Mary asked impetuously.

Sheriff Green waved at his boots, which were clearly soaked. His trousers, too, were wet to the knee. No wonder he was standing so close to the fire, he must be freezing!

"The water must have gone down some overnight," he said. "I convinced my horse to go through just on the flat side above where the bridge is – where the bridge was. There's a little wreckage, but you won't be able to tell any clues from that."

"Clues?" said George.

"I think you know what you're doing, George. If you shored it up just the day before, there must have been some reason why it didn't last."

George frowned and opened his mouth, and Sheriff Green raised a hand, forestalling any more questions.

"I can't tell you what's happening. I only have my suspicions, and it certainly isn't my place as an officer of the law to plant doubts in anyone's mind. Just keep your eyes open."

"Is that what you came for?" George asked him. "To warn me about the bridge?"

"No, I didn't even know about it until I got here. I came about something else." He hesitated, his eyes straying in Mary's direction. George followed his gaze and swallowed hard.

"Whatever it is, she needs to hear it, too," he said. "She's agreed to marry me, and I won't keep any secrets from her."

"Well, all right." With obvious reluctance, Sheriff Green dug in his pocket and pulled out a much-folded piece of paper. He undid the folds and handed it over to George. Mary stepped up beside her soon-to-be husband. One look at the paper, and she sucked in a deep breath.

It was a wanted poster, hand drawn. The man on the poster was the spitting image of George.

"This was delivered this morning," said Sheriff Green quietly. "Came with a note from the boys over outside of Dunnigan. Apparently, there was a witness to suspicious behavior from this individual, in the vicinity of the murder of Albert Shackleton."

George shook his head. "I already told you, Sheriff. I didn't know Albert Shackleton. I didn't know hardly anybody in Dunnigan."

Mary took the poster from him quietly and stared at the sketch.

"This is what you didn't want to tell me about?" she asked.

"Yes," said George. "I'm sorry, Mary, it was wrong of me to keep it from you. But you had only just arrived, and I was afraid that you would think you had made a mistake coming here." He scratched the back of his neck, eyeing the poster. "I guess you might still think that."

She looked up at him. "You claim your innocence?"

"I do. I did not kill that man. I've never hurt anybody."

"Then I believe you," she said simply, folded the poster up, and handed it back to the sheriff. "And that's all there is to it."

Sheriff Green shoved the poster back into his pocket.

"I wish that was all there was to it, ma'am," he said. "I'd like to believe George here, too. We don't know you well, George, but you've seemed to carry on a respectable life as long as you've been here, and we'd like to see you be successful here at the farm. But the fact of the matter is that evidence is piling up against you, evidence that doesn't look any too good. And there's no one else that has been pointed out, or at least, we'd have other options. Other lawmen are very concerned that the murderer might still be at large, and I'm inclined to understand their point of view, too."

George nodded. "I get it," he said. "It don't look good to maybe have a suspected murderer running around – especially with you running for re-election."

"Now, that's got nothing to do with it, George. That's the furthest thing from my mind. I just want to do my job the best I can."

"You say you don't know me well, Sheriff," George pointed out. "Well, I don't know you too well, neither. I want to believe that you want to do what's right. And that you won't try to bring me in just on someone's say-so. But there's obviously more going on here than I know about. So if you would lay your cards on the table, it would help me out. Who's pointing fingers at me? Is it Johnny Olsen?"

Sheriff Green shook his head.

"This goes far beyond Johnny Olsen," he said, and tapped his pocket where the poster was. "This is information from law enforcement in Dunnigan. I know Olsen's been a pain in the neck, but don't expect that if he quiets down, this will all go away."

George nodded, eyes falling away to the floor. "Well?" he said. "Do you need to take me in?"

"Not right now, George. Like I said, evidence is mounting, but I trust that you'll stay put here in town and not leave the area." He nodded at Mary. "Especially with a good woman like this to keep you in place."

"Fine. Can I have a few days to try and clear my name?"

"I'd appreciate all the help I can get on this, George."

The two men's gazes met at last, and they nodded slowly. Mary got the impression that they had reached an understanding, something that she herself did not quite grasp.

"I'll be on my way, then," said Sheriff Green, taking up his hat from where he had set it on the hearth. "Good day to you, Miss Mary."

He was gone, leaving the two of them together, standing close near the fire. Mary wrapped her arms about herself and shivered, and George's attention was drawn to her immediately.

"Still cold, are you?"

"No – yes – George, will you promise me that you are innocent?"

"Yes," he said, gently. "I promise you, Mary. And I promise that I will find a way to prove it. I'm not going to let something like this stop our wedding."

He held out a hand to her and, after a moment of hesitation, she took it.

"Now," he went on, "how about you go and make us some coffee. I need to head outside and see if I can rig up a way across the river, just something to keep us going until I can get the bridge rebuilt. There might be enough to at least make a dry spot for the horse to walk, even if we can't take the cart."

She nodded, turning to head back into the kitchen, but he forestalled her for a moment, holding tightly to her hand.

"And Mary…"

"Yes, George?"

He smiled. "I'm going to need some help decorating that tree."

CHAPTER 11

It just about broke George's heart to see how exhausted Mary looked as he left her in Annie's capable care. The ruckus of the day before, the fear and fright of falling into the river, the alarm of hearing of his encounter with the law, must all be combining to weigh heavily on her. Though they had only known each other a short time, he had already grown to view her as someone who could deal with anything that life threw at her. The first few weeks in Shallow Gorge were evidently determined to test that theory.

He had to leave her with Annie. As much as he wanted her to go with him, she was a distraction to him. And right now, he knew that no matter how friendly and concerned and honorable Sheriff Green was, or seemed to be, there was a time limit on how long he would let George roam free. The next bit of evidence that showed up could be enough to lock him up until there was a trial.

There must be more going on than he understood. It was obvious that Sheriff Green thought so, too, though he was reluctant to point fingers. Someone had drawn the wanted poster, that much was clear. Whether it was from Dunnigan as had been represented, or whether it was from somewhere closer, remained to be seen. And someone had dropped George's name to the law enforcement over in the mining settlement.

Did that have anything to do with George's bridge being tampered with? How could the two possibly connected? George couldn't see any link between them, but the fact that all of this was happening at once certainly made it seem unlikely that it all wasn't related. He just didn't have the sort of mind that could think of these things, that was all. He needed help.

He needed Jimmy.

Jimmy Goshawk was the only person that George had really known in the little mining settlement known as Dunnigan. This was simply and purely because everyone knew Jimmy. He ran the town's only drinking establishment, stocked almost entirely with alcohol of his own brew and make, strong enough to take the paint off a house and cheap enough to be bought in generous quantities. Jimmy was a wizened, thoughtful older man; when George first met Annie Borge, he was reminded of Jimmy, and had thought more than once of how well the two would get along together.

He had never expected to need to contact Jimmy for anything, but the time had evidently come, whether he'd expected it or not.

The next question, of course, was how to do it. He has of half a mind to leap back on his horse and head for Dunnigan in person. But it was a few day's trek away from Shallow Gorge, and he had promised Sheriff Green that he wouldn't leave the area. Besides, what would Mary think if he just took off for parts unknown? And in the snow?

No, he had to send a telegram. Luckily, Jimmy lived right in the little settlement of Dunnigan; if, like most of the prospectors in the area, he was actually out in the wilderness, George's chances of contacting him were quite low. But there was a little telegraph office set up, if George remembered correctly, not far from Jimmy's shanty saloon. It was intended for emergencies. George thought this qualified.

With this goal in mind, he headed off to town to send a telegram to Dunnigan, hoping that it would fall into the right hands. What he really needed, as far as he could tell, was a character witness. Sheriff Green had made quite a big deal over the fact that no one really knew George here in Shallow Gorge. Well, if someone who knew him was what was required, he couldn't do much better than Jimmy Goshawk. The man who poured the liquor always knew the most about the men who drank it.

On the strength of that thought, after he sent the telegram on its way, George found his way into the Golden Apple, the little saloon that Shallow Gorge boasted on the main street. He was not a frequenter of the saloon, but after the last few days he'd had, the thought of a mid-afternoon whiskey was very attractive. Besides, the skies were taking on that silvery light that they got just before snow started to fall, and the temperature had dropped yet again. It never failed to astound George, how quickly the weather could change here during the winter.

It was only three days until Christmas. He would have to repair the bridge in order to get supplies and bring Mary back to the house again.

He was thinking deeply on this, turning his glass around and around, when someone slapped him heartily on the back and said, "Told you that bridge was dangerous."

How on earth had Johnny Olsen been able to hear what he was thinking? George looked up at him, squinting. The last thing he wanted at the moment was to have Olsen for a drinking buddy. But Olsen seemed determined to be friendly, taking a seat right next to him and waving at the bartender.

"Everything turned out all right, though," he said. "I heard no one was hurt, thank goodness."

"Yeah," said George. "No one was hurt."

"That pretty little girl of yours could come down with the croup, though, if you're not careful."

George glared at him, but Olsen was blithely tucking into the full glass that had just been placed in front of him.

"I wish you'd leave her out of it."

"I'm just showing a neighborly concern, like any good man would do," Olsen assured him. "I hear there's a warrant out for you."

George sat bolt upright. "What?"

"I think it's brave of you to sit right out here in public, mind you. Don't make them have to chase you down – it's the next best thing to going down to the sheriff's office and turning yourself in."

"Who told you there was a warrant out for me?"

"Oh, a little birdie," said Olsen, smiling. "I never reveal my sources, McDonald. Did you think any more about my proposition about the land? I have a feeling you're going to need my help – and you might regret it if you don't take advantage of it now."

George shook his head. "What is it? Is it my land you want? You want my whole farm, Olsen?"

Johnny Olsen didn't deign to reply, instead taking a deep draught from his glass, and waving again to the barkeep.

"Think about it," he advised. "You're running low on time." He glanced back behind him and grinned a swift and foxlike grin. "In fact, you might be out of it entirely."

George spun around in his seat. Sheriff Green had just entered the Golden Apple, and was advancing on him, one hand at his hip, near his holstered pistol.

"George McDonald," he said levelly, "I just received a warrant for your arrest."

George shot a quick glance at Olsen, who stared insolently back. He stood up, slowly, hands out and clearly empty. He could picture Olsen rooting for him to be shot by accident.

"I sent a telegram to a friend in Dunnigan," he said. "I'm waiting to hear back. He can tell you about my reputation, about where I was prospecting, about the day I brought my first gold in, about the day I left. He can tell you anything you want to know."

"I'll keep an eye out for him," said Sheriff Green levelly. His face was set and hard, but George could detect just a hint of regret in his voice. He held out his hand for George's arm. "Are you going to come quietly?"

George cast one last quick glance back at Olsen, who waited expectantly.

"Yes," he said. "Yes, I'll come quietly."

He waited until they had left the saloon, left Olsen behind, until he said, "I think Olsen has something to do with it."

"Now, you're just saying that because you don't like the man. I don't either, George, but that doesn't mean he's setting you up."

"Then he's not the one who gave you the tip about me living in Dunnigan before?"

Sheriff Green stayed silent, walking George down the road toward the law office – with the waiting empty jail cell. George heaved a sigh.

"Maybe that telegram will come in from Jimmy. That's the only way I know how to prove my innocence."

"I hope so, George."

They were at the office now. The jail cell loomed.

"Will you tell Mary where I am?" George asked quietly. "I'd hate for her to worry when I don't show up tomorrow."

"I'll tell her," Sheriff Green promised. "I think she's going to worry about you no matter, but I'll tell her."

At least there was that taken care of. Now, there was nothing to do but wait.

CHAPTER 12

Sheriff Green was as good as his word, because the next afternoon, Mary Ferguson showed up at the jail, with Annie Borge in tow. The young woman rushed past the deputy who let them in, hurrying to the single jail cell with her arm outstretched.

"George."

He reached through the bars, and she took his hands, holding them tightly.

"Mary, I'm so sorry about this."

"George, when are they going to let you out?"

He shook his head. "I don't know. They don't know, neither – no one can be sure how long this will go on. But I'm hoping that some evidence shows up to clear me, right soon."

To his distress, she appeared to be fighting back tears.

"George, this is awful. I was so worried when you didn't come back last night, and I thought maybe something else had happened with the bridge and the river – and then Sheriff Green came by this morning and that was almost worse, hearing that you had been arrested. George, I need you to know that I believe you. I believe in your innocence – I believe that you didn't hurt anyone."

He clutched her hands all the more tightly, and his gaze strayed beyond her to Annie Borge, who nodded gravely.

"I believe you too, George. But you know as well as I do that what we believe doesn't matter a whit. The only thing that matters is the evidence."

"I'm trying to do something about that, Annie. The evidence against me isn't good, but it isn't conclusive, either. They just need someone to vouch for me, is all." He tried to make it sound simple, as though it were the work of a moment to dig this new evidence up, though he knew that it was far more complicated than that. They needed a character witness, it was true, but they also needed proof that he was being framed. Otherwise, there was nothing to prove that he hadn't been anywhere near the man who had been shot, let alone near his stolen gold.

He was sure that Annie understood this, but he was reluctant to spell it out any more clearly for Mary. She was already very upset; he hated that he was the one who had caused her misery.

She dropped his hands and turned to the basket she had brought, which she had set hastily on the floor just inside the door when she entered.

"We brought you some food – if that's all right," she added, turning to the deputy for confirmation. Deputy Jones came forward, took the cloth off the top of the basket, and poked around inside for a moment before nodding.

"Looks all right to me," he said, and grinned. "As a matter of fact, if you brought enough for two…"

"Oh," Mary gave a short, distracted chuckle, and fished a corn muffin out from the basket to hand to him. Then she took a few paper-wrapped parcels from the basket and pushed them through the bars to George. "I don't know what they feed you in here."

"Oh, I'm all right, Mary, thank you." He took the food, nonetheless. It was still warm and smelled delightful. "You didn't have to go through all this trouble."

"I wanted to do something," said Mary, her voice small. "After Sheriff Green came by, I – I couldn't just sit and do nothing. I was going crazy." She looked up at him, eyes swimming with tears. "I hate seeing you like this, George."

He hated it, too. "I don't want to upset you," he said quietly. "I want to make you happy."

"And you will. When you're set free and we get married, George, I'll be the happiest woman around."

He stared at her, wonderingly.

"I believe you mean it, too," he said softly. He had never seen a woman look at him the way she was looking at him now. If he knew anything at all, that look was the look of love. Mary Ferguson was in love with him.

And she wasn't alone in her feelings, either. His pulse quickened, even though things looked mighty bleak.

Annie tapped Mary on the shoulder. Today, unlike every day in the past week, had started out cloudy and continued to get darker. The wind outside the little jail was whipping up, moaning around the corners. There was a good, solid storm on the way, and they had to get back before it struck.

Mary turned back to George. She pressed his hand through the bars, biting her lip.

"I'll be back tomorrow," she promised.

"Tomorrow," said George. He shook his head. "Tomorrow is the day before Christmas Eve. I don't even think that Sheriff Green will be here."

"I'll work it out somehow." She cast a glance at the deputy, who gave a shrug. "I'll bring more corn muffins, or something."

George couldn't help himself; he grinned.

"Might need a little more than that. Try some fritters, maybe."

She laughed, and he was pleased to see it. "Good night, George."

"Good night, Mary."

He watched her as she left the law post, wishing that he could be with her, holding her hand, feeling her warmth. The door closed behind them, and opened again almost immediately, this time allowing a much less appealing figure to pass: Johnny Olsen. He strolled up to Deputy Jones' desk and tapped on it.

"Evening, Harry."

"Evening, Johnny."

"I guess you've got the worst job of 'em all, eh?"

Deputy Jones shrugged, leaning back in his chair. "Not too bad. He's been no trouble."

"Really? Such a surprise, considering he's wanted for murder." Olsen turned to the jail cell and fixed his cold eyes on George. "Might I have a word with him?"

"Talking's free in this country," said Deputy Jones. Olsen nodded, and strode forward. George leaned against the cell bars, dangling his hands out, eyeing the man.

"What is it that you want?"

"Oh, just here to offer my help as a friend, of course." Olsen put a hand on his heart, fervently – and falsely, George knew. "It seems that the worst has come to pass, and you've been jailed. Now, I hate to see you in a position like this."

"Yeah, I bet you do."

"So I thought I'd come one more time and make my offer. I can take care of your land, if you sign it over to me. I won't even ask for anything in return. And if it's poor Miss Mary you're most worried about, why, I can help with that, too." He grinned widely. "I saw her leaving just now. Such a pretty little thing. It's a shame that you'll miss sitting around the fire with her come Christmas Eve."

George stared at him. "Three times," he said. "That's three times that you tried to get me to give up my land. You knew that I lived in Dunnigan – you knew about the warrant. It's you, ain't it, Olsen? You're the one who's trying to set me up."

Olsen glanced over at Deputy Jones, who appeared only mildly interested. "Whoa there, McDonald."

"Yeah, you can't just throw around accusations like that," said Olsen snidely.

"Why not? You done exactly the same thing. You told Sheriff Green about my past – why, I wouldn't be surprised to find that you drew that wanted poster yourself!"

"Hang on, now," interjected Jones at last, standing up. "Don't get too excited, George."

"Don't you hear what I'm saying?" said George loudly. "He's set me up, Deputy Jones. He wants my land and he thinks this is the way to get it."

Jones shook his head, and Olsen folded his arms, fixing George with a sickening grin.

"It's sad, what a little jail time does to a man's brain," he said. "I hope that you can clear yourself, McDonald. Between one thing and another, you stand to lose everything you've ever had – including the gold you stole from Shackleton."

George pressed even harder against the bars, arms out straight through them, reaching for Olsen. If he could just grab the man and get his hands around his neck, maybe he would be singing a different tune. But Olsen stayed well out of reach, shaking his head and tsk-tsking like a disappointed grandmother.

"Well, I'd better be on my way," he said languidly. "I've got a few more calls to pay this evening. I just wanted to wish you well, McDonald. In the spirit of Christmas, and all."

When he went out the door, he was laughing.

CHAPTER 13

Mary slept badly that night, tossing and turning and thinking of George alone in his cell. In the morning, she awoke with swollen eyes and an aching heart. It was the day before Christmas Eve, and she was filled with a horrible suspicion that George would still be stuck in that lonely little cell, come Christmas morning.

Annie gave her a cup of hot tea and sat down next to her at the kitchen table in what had quickly become their morning routine.

"Don't fret, dear," she said, kindly. "You and I both believe that George is innocent. The truth will come to light, somehow."

Mary leaned her chin on her hand.

"How?" she said hopelessly. "The murder apparently happened days away from here. How can we find the proof of what happened?"

Annie shook her head. "We don't need to know exactly what happened," she said. "That's up to the law enforcement at the mining camp. All we need to know is how to show that it wasn't George that did it."

"But he says himself that there was no one around who could give him an alibi."

"I know, dear. It looks bad – it's difficult, for sure. But difficult is not the same thing as impossible. Have a little faith."

Mary let out a heartfelt sigh. "I'm trying to," she said. "Especially at this time of year, I want to think good of others. But more than anything, I want the man I'm going to marry out of jail and here by my side."

They sat for a few moments more in silence, each woman thinking her own thoughts.

Later in the morning, Annie consented to drive Mary into town again, in the hopes that there would be someone at the jail to let her visit with George.

"I can't stand the thought of him just sitting there on his own," she confessed. "Even if I all I can do is wave at him through the window, it's better than nothing."

"Let's get him a fruitcake from the general store," suggested Annie. "Nothing cheers a body up around Christmas time like a good fruitcake."

The suggestion was a good one, and so they stopped at the general store before they headed to the jail. As Annie hemmed and hawed over which fruitcake would be the best to take to a jailed prisoner for his pre-Christmas Eve treat, Mary found herself drawn to the few racks of ready-made dresses in the corner. There was one that was a pale blue silk, as pretty as a winter sky here in Colorado, and she couldn't help but pass her fingers over it, finding the texture soothing. She could have a dress like this as her wedding gown – if she ever got married. If her husband to be was ever let out of jail, with his name cleared –

A voice filtered through the little daydream that she had entered, a familiar voice. She couldn't quite place it at first. It was charming, ingratiating, but there was a quality about it that she didn't like. She found the source of the voice, a man with jet black hair and a thick black mustache. It was not a familiar face to her, and she wandered a little closer, frowning in concentration, trying to figure out where she had met the man before.

"I don't think there's anything wrong with volunteering to help a neighbor out," he was saying to the man behind the counter. The store owner appeared dubious, and it was clear that the black-haired man was trying to worm him into doing something. There was a wheedling, persuasive tone to his words. "And George is my neighbor, you know."

That alone would have made her perk up. She realized abruptly where she had heard the man's voice before – he was the one who had visited George the very first day that she had gone to the farmhouse. His name was Olsen, Johnny Olsen. George hadn't liked him, and she could understand why. Even without knowing him, she didn't like him either.

"Well, I know that," said the store owner, a little peevishly. "I'm not saying that it wouldn't be helpful. I'm just saying, when George came in here to send off his telegram, he seemed very anxious to make sure that it got where it was going. And since the reply came so quick, it makes me think it must be important."

"Sure, it is," said Johnny Olsen. "And, like I said, I'll see that he gets it immediately. Why, I'm headed that direction myself right this minute." He held out a hand. "If it's so important, I can't see why you'd want to wait until he comes in here after it. Besides, he's not really free to be fetching telegrams right now."

The store owner hesitated a moment longer, and then finally relented and gave Olsen a folded piece of yellow paper.

"This is what I get for not having clear-cut rules even though we're the only place in town with access to a telegraph," he said ruefully. "If my wife was here, I'd head off and deliver it myself, but I'm alone today and overworked."

"Don't think a thing of it," said Olsen, swiftly pocketing the paper. "Just call me your errand boy. In fact, I'll take it to him now. Don't even thank me. It's a hobby of mine, doing things for other people." Still yammering on in his slimy way, he oozed back out the front door. Mary watched him go, suspiciously.

A telegram for George. That had to be important. She needed to ask him about it immediately.

Just her luck – Annie appeared at her elbow, holding a fruitcake, ready to pay for it at the counter.

"Are you finally ready?" she asked, grinning.

Mary nodded. "Let's hurry, please," she said.

And hurry they did, indeed, leaving the cart where it was and walking swiftly down the street to the sheriff's office, which housed the jail as well. Mary was relieved to find that Sheriff Green was, in fact, in the office. He seemed to be expecting them, in fact, and got up to greet them when they came in.

"Thought you might show up today," he said. "I wouldn't normally be here on a day like this, but George was sure that you would come."

"Yes," said Mary, glancing past him anxiously to see George, standing at the cell door, holding onto the bars with both hands and clearly waiting for her. "May I see him now?"

"Sure, come on in."

She took the fruitcake from Annie, without even asking, and stepped past the sheriff, leaving the two others behind. Out of consideration for her obvious desire for privacy, she was glad to see that they stepped out fully into the outer office and closed the door behind them, leaving her alone in the inner office, next to the solitary jail cell.

She rushed forward, pushing the little cake through the bars for him to take.

"Good afternoon, Mary," he said warmly. His eyes were aglow. "I'm so glad to see you again."

"I said I'd come, didn't it?"

"I know, but I still wasn't sure if it would work out. After all – it's not your fault that I'm stuck in here. The last thing you want to do is spend all of your Christmas in a jail cell."

"You're right," she said. "I don't want to do that, so we'd better get you out. Tell me, George, who would send you a telegram?"

His head snapped up, his eyes suddenly very alert. "A telegram?"

"I was in the general store, and the owner was saying that you sent one off yesterday."

"I did, yes."

"And you got one in return, today. You got it, didn't you?"

He set the cake down on the floor abruptly and put both hands out, palms up.

"Do you have it? Will you give it to me, Mary?"

"I don't have it," she admitted, blushing. "The store owner doesn't know me from anyone, he certainly wouldn't have given it to me. Your neighbor Johnny Olsen had a difficult enough time convincing him to hand it over to him. He said he would bring it right here."

"Johnny Olsen!"

"Yes – what was in the telegram, George?"

George was breathing quickly. "I don't know exactly," he said, "but if Olsen got it, it must be good for me and bad for him. We've got to get it back from him – it's what will prove that I'm innocent. I'm sure of it." He gripped the bars, twisting his hands and tightening them until his knuckles went white. "Will you get Sheriff Green, Mary, and tell him what happened? Hurry!"

She nodded and ducked back out of the room. To her distress, however, both Annie and the sheriff were nowhere to be seen in the outer room. She hurried outside and found that they were nowhere to be seen on the street, either. Mary gave vent to a little cry of distress, wringing her hands. Where could they have gone?

It was freezing cold and getting darker by the moment as the clouds piled up. They must have thought that she and George needed a little more alone time – perhaps they went to get a cup of tea or something stronger at the saloon. She hadn't been there, yet, but she knew where it was. There was a sign hanging from the building down on the corner, swinging in the wind. The Golden Apple.

It was her best bet.

She hurried, hoping against hope that she would find the sheriff, and that the sheriff would find Olsen, and that they would be in time before the telegram was destroyed. What might Olsen do with the telegram? She had no idea. Likely it depended on what the telegram actually said.

Whatever the case, if it was something that would set George free, she would find it. She had to. As she hurried, she wondered whether the telegram operator would remember what the telegram had said. Would he be able to help? She had no idea. The best thing was to get the actual telegram back. She began to feel frantic as her heart pounded hard against her ribs.

She plunged through the swinging doors of the Golden Apple and froze. This early in the afternoon, there were only a few people there. The first one she saw was Johnny Olsen.

He looked up from his glass as she came in, and she knew by the smile that crossed his face that he knew exactly who she was. She bit her lip and held her breath and walked slowly toward him.

Once she was a few feet away, she stopped, and said in a rush, "Mr. Olsen, I need that telegram from you, and I need it now."

Olsen glanced casually back at his drink, as though it were far more interesting than any strange woman showing up and making demands of him.

"What telegram?"

"I know you have it. I was there when you got it from the general store."

Olsen closed his eyes and sighed. "I can't imagine what it matters to you," he said. "You only just met McDonald – why are you so invested in setting him free?"

She swallowed hard. "Not that it's any of your business," she said, "but we are going to be married."

Olsen stared pointblank at her and raised his eyebrows.

"A wedding in the jailhouse," he said ruminatively. "Fascinating." He dug in his pocket and brought out a folded slip of yellow paper. "But what does this telegram even contain, Miss Mary? How do you know that whether it's good news or bad? Suppose it only proves that your beloved is guilty of murder? What would you say then?"

"It must be good," she said levelly, "or you wouldn't have stolen it."

He considered this for a moment, then inclined his head politely.

"Perhaps," he said. He glanced up at the barkeep, who was standing watching them with his arms folded. "Let's go and have a seat by the fireplace, and talk this over like civilized people," Olsen suggested.

He stood up from his bar stool, and she stepped forward. Perhaps if she leapt at him, timing it just right, she could take him by surprise and wrest the paper from him. Perhaps she could trip him as he walked, and pounce on him while he was on the floor and get it from him like that. A hundred thoughts and a hundred plans flashed through her mind, all of them tainted by the knowledge that he was far, far bigger than her, and that there was really very little she could do.

Except talk.

"Very well," she said, trying to keep her heart from her throat. Taking a deep breath, she followed him.

CHAPTER 14

Sheriff Mike Green, accompanied by Annie Borge, came back into the back room of the sheriff's office, laughing at his own joke. He stopped cold as he looked up and realized that Mary Ferguson was nowhere to be seen.

George pushed against the bars. "Where is Mary? Did you see her? Did you get it?"

"Did I get what?"

"The telegram!"

"Where did Mary go?" asked Annie.

"She went in search of you," bellowed George, balling his hands into fists. Sheriff Green held his own hands up.

"Now, hold on, hold on. No need to get all excited. Just calm down, George, and tell me what happened."

With a mighty effort, George got control of himself and explained what had occurred. Annie's face went pale.

"That's why she was so anxious to leave the general store," she said. "Curse that man."

"Now, Annie," admonished Sheriff Green. "We don't even know what the telegram said."

"That's true, Mike, but you can bet your boots that if it helped out poor George here, that snake of a neighbor will hide it from you. I'm no lawman, but it looks to me like everything George suspected is true. Johnny Olsen is setting him up, out to get whatever he can." Annie put her hands on her hips. "Now, are you going to stand there and talk about proof, or are you going to let this man out and go and get it?"

Sheriff Green hesitated a second, He looked from Annie to George, and then shook his head.

"All right," he said. "Truth is, I believe he's innocent. It's certainly not regulation, but I'm thinking sometimes rules can be broke. I believe you, George. Let's go get him."

He let George out of the cell and had to stand back to avoid being run over as the young farmer rushed forward. Once out on the street, in the gathering gloom from the storm, George looked up and down the street, frowning heavily.

"Where do you suppose she went?"

"We just came back from the store," said Annie. "I was showing Mike the type of fruitcake that keeps the best. So I don't know that she went that direction."

"But she could have," pointed out Sheriff Green. "Maybe we just didn't see her."

George nodded, reaching a snap decision. "Fine. You two go that way, and I'll go this way. If we don't find her in half an hour, we meet back here at the jail." He strode off in his chosen direction.

At the edge of his hearing, he was vaguely aware that he caught Annie, somewhere behind him, saying admiringly, "Love does good things to a man, don't you think, Mike?"

He made it to the corner in just a few moments, and was hesitating on which way to go next, looking left and right, when the barkeep stepped out of the saloon right next to him and yanked on his sleeve.

"Hey, you're George McDonald, ain't you?"

"Yeah."

"You're the subject of much discussion in here. I'd get inside if I was you, before the little lady scratches Olsen's eyes out."

George's heart leapt into his throat. He pushed past the barkeeper and rushed into the saloon, eyes frantically searching out Mary's figure. In the corner, he saw her, sitting next to the fire, bolt upright, hands in her lap, eyes wide and aflame with anger. Next to her, leaning in, one hand reaching out and nearly touching her knee, was none other than Johnny Olsen.

George was in the middle of them before he even knew that he had moved. The heat of the blazing fire was scorching on him after the frigid cold outside, and he could hear Mary gasp behind him. Johnny Olsen looked up at him, and slowly stood, coming up to his full height.

"You escaped, I see," he observed.

"I was let out," said George, tightly. "It seems some new evidence has come to light."

He could feel Mary's presence right at his back, almost but not quite touching him.

"It's in his pocket, George," she whispered.

"New evidence?" said Olsen. He brought out the folded piece of paper and held it up. "This, you mean?" He examined it lazily, as though he'd never even seen it before. "Why, you don't even know what it says. It could be evidence for you… or it could be evidence against. Who's to say?"

"Sheriff Green will have something to say about it, I expect," said George grimly. He reached out a hand. "Give it to me."

But before he could so much as move, or yell, Olsen had balled the yellow paper up and flung it into the fire, where it caught alight immediately and blazed into ash in a matter of seconds. Olsen grinned.

"Guess we'll never know."

George heard Mary give a small yelp and felt her grab at his arm. It was true, he had taken another step toward Olsen – but he stopped himself there.

"The truth will come out," he said. "I'm an innocent man, and nothing you can do will change that."

Olsen sneered.

"Oh, yeah? We'll just have to wait and see about that – Mary and I can wait right here by the fire, and you can do your waiting back in your cold, little jail cell."

From just inside the saloon, where he had entered without anyone's noticing, Sheriff Green said, "I don't think that will be necessary."

The look of shock on Olsen's face was something that George would treasure forever. Even better, however, was the expression that appeared when the sheriff took Olsen's arms behind his back and put his wrists in handcuffs.

"You're under arrest, Johnny Olsen."

Olsen sputtered.

"What? What? You can't do this! This is a miscarriage of justice! Arrest on what grounds?"

"Oh, impeding a lawful investigation," said Sheriff Green. "Sowing false rumors to try and get an innocent man arrested. Probably sabotaging a bridge and endangering the lives of others." He grinned at Mary and George. "Trying to incite trouble right here in the saloon."

"How do you know?" said George. "He burned the telegram."

"Luckily, Mr. Owen at the general store keeps a copy when they come through. I don't expect you two know that, but I do – because I'm the sheriff. It's my job to know these things."

He set a newly handcuffed Olsen back down in his chair, and put his hands on his hips, nodding at George.

"It was from your friend Jimmy Goshawk in Dunnigan. Jimmy's apparently well known to the local sheriff and went up to vouch for your character. That was helpful enough, but what's even better is that he mentioned that a week or so ago, he got a visit from a tall man with pitch black hair and a very noticeable fringe – gave his name as O'Leary, but we all know who it really was. Evidently, he was asking questions about you, George, finding out your history, and discovered enough to plant some doubt in the minds of the local law.

Guess you've got something he wants, and he thought this was how to get it from you."

George looked down at Olsen and shook his head. Olsen stared into the fire, refusing to meet anyone's gaze, until Sheriff Green took him by the arm and hauled him upright.

"It's a shame I've got to arrest you right before Christmas Eve," he said. "Looks like you're gonna to be spending the holiday alone." He tipped his hat. "George. Miss Mary."

Then they were gone, leaving George and Mary by the fire. George collapsed into Olsen's recently vacated chair and stared at his fiancée, who stared back at him. She looked just as exhausted as he felt.

"Well, there you have it," she said. "The end of the adventure – and just in time, too. I still intend to cook a Christmas turkey."

He laughed. He couldn't help it.

"I'm afraid the adventure has just begun," he said. "It ain't easy to live here in Shallow Gorge – I haven't been here much longer than you, Mary, but I can swear to it, if you'll trust me."

"I do," she said simply. He leaned forward.

"The message from Jimmy was a big help," he said, "but it wasn't the same as an alibi. There's no way for me to prove that I wasn't around when Shackleton was shot."

"You don't need to prove anything to me."

"You believe me, then?"

"I do," said Mary. "You always said that you weren't the type of man who hurt others, and I believe it with all my heart.

When Olsen burnt that telegram, you didn't even try to hit him. Any other man would have – I certainly would have." She took his hands and held them firmly, smiling up at him. "It's a good thing you were there to restrain me, or I'd be spending Christmas in the jail cell myself."

He gripped her hands tightly, returning her smile. "I'm glad things worked out the way they did," he said. "We've still got the rest of today before Christmas Eve, and – Mary."

"Yes, George?"

"I really need some help with decorating that tree."

Mary Ferguson laughed.

"Come on, then, Mr. McDonald," she said, standing up and holding her hand out to him.

Annie, who up until that minute had kept quiet, said, "It looks like snow any minute, and you've got a lot to do. Let's be getting home."

They all laughed.

"You and your weather reports," George said, smiling fondly at Annie.

He stood, took Mary's hand, and pressed a kiss to the back of it. "We do have a lot to get done. We got a holiday to celebrate, a wedding to plan, and a life to start, together."

Mary smiled shyly at him and nodded.

"And a life to start together," she repeated, her voice soft with happiness.

The End

CONTINUE READING...

Thank you for reading *The Christmas Groom's Innocence!* **Are you wondering what to read next?** Why not read *Christmas in Shallow Gorge?* **Here's a peek for you:**

At half past six on a crystal-clear December morning, Billy Spence woke up with a sudden feeling of dread. He didn't normally sleep in so late – with the children and the farm, there was always so much to do, he couldn't afford it. But the night before he'd been up late with Liddy, and evidently the exhaustion had caught up to him.

But it wasn't the lateness of the hour that had woken him – it was the surety that something was terribly wrong. He sat up in his narrow bed and listened to the sounds of the house. Nothing unusual, nothing out of place – the children must still be abed, for which he was grateful. He hated to think that his sleeping in had kept them from something they needed.

It would be so much simpler if there was someone else in the house, so much easier to make sure that his three little ones were cared for – but he shook the thought out of his head. There was no use mourning over something that had changed years ago.

Marian was gone, lost to him and their children forever nothing could bring her back.

He pushed that thought, too, ruthlessly out of his mind, and threw back the covers at the same time. It was freezing, the hard wood floor little more than an icy sheet beneath his bare feet. He fumbled into his trousers and pulled on a shirt, still driven by the feeling that something was wrong. The fire must have gone out, even though he had banked it so carefully the evening before. It was far colder in the house than it should have been.

Emerging into the hall, he glanced first to the right, to see that the door to the children's room was still shut, and then to the left, toward the sitting room and the entryway. Everything looked fine from where he was, so he moved toward the kitchen, which was in the front corner of the house. Just as he was about to pass through the doorway, he glanced once more toward the entry, and froze.

The door was open. The front door was ajar – not much, but certainly enough to let in the cold air—and wolves, had any animals decided to investigate.

Billy used some harsh words on himself as he hurried to the front and closed the door firmly. How could he be so absent-minded? Of course, he had been tired the previous evening, but that was hardly an excuse for risking his family.

On the thought, he moved back through the house toward his children's shared bedroom.

Visit HERE To Read More!
http://ticahousepublishing.com/mail-order-brides.html

ABOUT THE AUTHOR

Susannah has always been intrigued with the Western movement - prairie days, mail-order brides, the gold rush, frontier life! As a writer, she's excited to combine her love of story with her love of all that is Western. Presently, Susannah lives in Wyoming with her hubby and their three amazing children.

www.ticahousepublishing.com
contact@ticahousepublishing.com